I Wonder Why
Fish Grew Legs

and other questions about prehistoric life

Jackie Gaff

KINGFISHER
BOSTON

KINGFISHER
a Houghton Mifflin Company imprint
222 Berkeley Street
Boston, Massachusetts 02116
www.houghtonmifflinbooks.com

First published in hardcover in 2001
First published in this format in 2004
10 9 8 7 6 5 4 3 2 1
1TR/0204/SHE/RNB/126.6MA(F)

Copyright © Kingfisher Publications Plc 2001

LIBRARY OF CONGRESS CATALOGING-IN-PUBLICATION DATA
has been applied for.

ISBN 978-0-7534-5762-7

Printed in Taiwan

Series designer: David West
    Children's Books
Author: Jackie Gaff
Consultant: Steve Parker
Illustrations: James Field (SGA) 12, 14–15, 16–17,
18–19, 20–21, 22–23, 24–25, 26–27; Andrew
Harland (SGA) 7b, 10–11: Mike Lacey (SGA) 4–5,
29, 30–31; Sarah Smith (SGA) 6–7t, 7b, 8t, 9b, 13;
Stephen Sweet (SGA) 4t, 5b; Ross Walton (SGA) 6b,
8b, 8–9t, 28; Peter Wilkes (SGA) all cartoons.

CONTENTS

What is prehistory?

Prehistory is the time before people began to record in writing the things that happened to them and in the world around them. It is the story of Earth from its birth to the invention of writing, about 5,500 years ago.

● The first true writing system was invented by people called the Sumerians, who lived in the area we now call the Middle East.

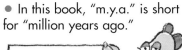

● In this book, "m.y.a." is short for "million years ago."

m.y.a.

● Earth formed about 4,600 m.y.a. from a cloud of dust and gas spinning around the Sun.

- Before the scientific study of fossils began in the late 1700s, some people thought fossils were real animals that had been turned into stone by hot sunlight.

How do we know about prehistoric life?

People who study prehistoric life work like detectives, slowly piecing clues together from fossils—the stony remains of animals and plants that died millions of years ago.

- Most fossils formed after a dead plant or animal sank to the bottom of a river, lake, or sea and was covered by layers of sand or mud.

- Over millions of years the sand and mud hardened into rock, with the animal or plant buried inside as a stony fossil.

When did life on Earth begin?

Earth was a boiling hot mass of rock at first. Millions of years passed before its surface cooled down enough for life to survive. The first living things may have appeared as long as 4,000 m.y.a., but so far scientists have not found fossils to prove this. The earliest known fossils belong to tiny, microscopic bacteria that lived in the oceans about 3,500 m.y.a.

- The first many-celled creatures looked a little like worms, jellyfish, and sea anemones. Their bodies were soft and squishy, without bones or shells.

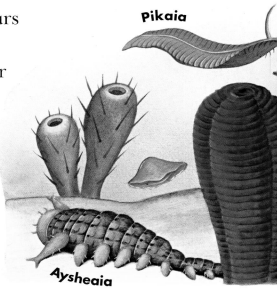

Pikaia

Aysheaia

- In some places the bacteria clustered together into matlike sheets, which built up into mounds called stromatolites. Over time the stromatolites became fossils.

Stromatolites

What is evolution?

Evolution is what scientists call the gradual change of one kind of living thing into another. It happens very, very slowly. The first bacteria were tiny single cells. It took more than 2.5 billion years for the earliest known larger creatures, with bodies made up of many cells, to evolve.

Eldonia

Hallucigenia

● Measuring 2 feet (60cm) across, Dickinsonia was as wide as a swimming ring.

What is extinction?

Not all living things carry on evolving. Sometimes a particular kind of animal or plant dies out and disappears from Earth completely. This is extinction.

Trilobite

● Trilobites evolved at least 600 m.y.a. and became extinct about 240 m.y.a. They were among the first animals to have eyes, and they were some of the earliest to have bodies protected by a tough, shell-like exoskeleton.

When did fish appear in the oceans?

Sacabambaspis

When fish evolved about 500 m.y.a., they were the first animals to have real backbones. They had no jaws or fins, however, and looked much like modern-day tadpoles.

Climatius

- With no jaws for biting or chewing, early fish like Arandaspis fed by sucking up tiny creatures from the seabed.

Cladoselache

Cheirolepis

- Dunkleosteus was a whopping 18 feet (6m) long, but it wasn't a shark. This scary monster belonged to a group called the armored fish, because of the bony plates that protected their heads from attackers' teeth.

Dunkleosteus

Were sharks around in prehistoric times?

They certainly were—sharks were cruising the oceans by about 400 m.y.a. They were among the earliest of the backboned animals to develop jaws and hard teeth, and they were just as ferocious as today's sharks!

● You wouldn't want to go swimming with Stethacanthus. The top of this early shark's weird, T-shaped fin was covered in teethlike bristles, and so was its head.

What were the sea scorpions?

The sea scorpions were fierce hunters with barbed claws for snatching up their food. They lived at the same time as the early sharks and grew to 6 feet (2m) long. They did not have a backbone. Instead, their bodies were covered by a shell-like exoskeleton.

Pterygotus

When did plants get a foothold on land?

Plants were successful on land before animals were, and the earliest known fossils of a land plant date back to about 420 m.y.a. Scientists call the plant Cooksonia, and it was tiny—about as long as your little finger.

Protocarus

● Although Cooksonia had a stem, it didn't have leaves, flowers, or proper roots.

Diplopodan

Why were prehistoric plants important?

The arrival of land plants meant that there was enough food around for land animals to evolve too. Among the first to eat up their greens were tiny mites and insects such as springtails.

● All animals need oxygen to survive. Because plants use the Sun's energy to turn carbon dioxide into oxygen, they helped to increase the air's oxygen levels.

- Once plant-eating land animals were around, meat-eaters evolved to munch on them.

Mesaraneus

Why did fish pop their heads above water?

Most fish take oxygen from the water through their gills. But after land plants appeared, something weird happened—some kinds of fish developed lungs for breathing air. Scientists call them lungfish and think they evolved because there wasn't enough oxygen in the shallow rivers and lakes where they lived.

Eusthenopteron

- The weather became much warmer at the time that lungfish evolved. Water evaporated and turned into vapor or gas, making lakes and rivers shallower, with less oxygen.

Why did fish grow legs?

Some fish didn't just grow lungs—their fins became legs, and they evolved into land animals! The earliest four-legged animals, Acanthostega and Ichthyostega, appeared about 370 m.y.a. They spent most of their time in the water, but they could crawl around on land.

● Acanthostega and Ichthyostega were ancestors of the amphibians—animals that can live on land, but lay their eggs in water.

Ichthyostega

Acanthostega

● Diplocaulus was a bizarre early amphibian with a boomerang-shaped head. It lived mainly underwater, where its head worked like a submarine's hydrofoils.

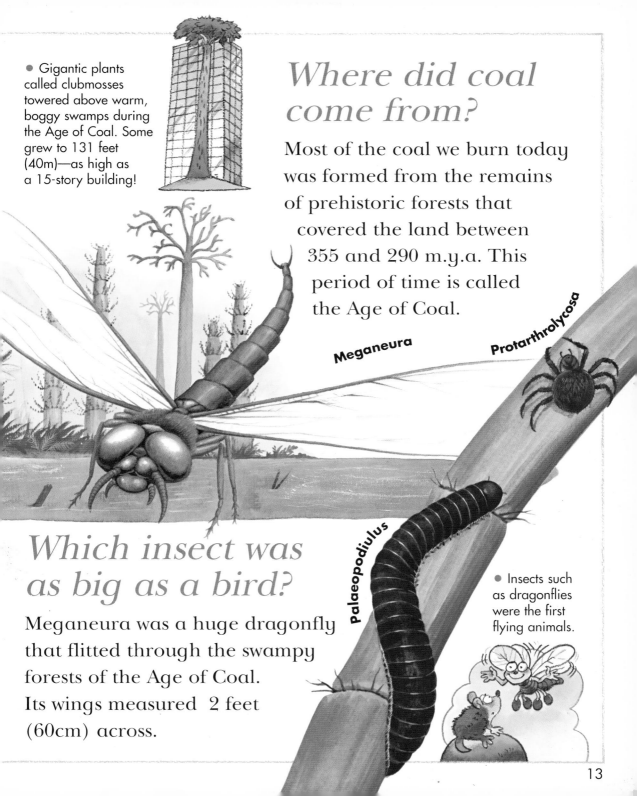

• Gigantic plants called clubmosses towered above warm, boggy swamps during the Age of Coal. Some grew to 131 feet (40m)—as high as a 15-story building!

Where did coal come from?

Most of the coal we burn today was formed from the remains of prehistoric forests that covered the land between 355 and 290 m.y.a. This period of time is called the Age of Coal.

Meganeura

Protarthrolycosa

Palaeopodiulus

Which insect was as big as a bird?

Meganeura was a huge dragonfly that flitted through the swampy forests of the Age of Coal. Its wings measured 2 feet (60cm) across.

• Insects such as dragonflies were the first flying animals.

13

When did reptiles appear?

Reptiles were a new group of animals that evolved from amphibians toward the end of the Age of Coal. Reptiles such as Hylonomus were the first four-legged animals to live in dry places where there was little water.

Hylonomus

• Reptiles have dry, scaly skin, and their eggs don't dry out because each egg is protected by a leathery shell.

• Amphibian eggs have no shells, so they have to be laid in water to stop them from drying out.

Which animals grew sails?

It isn't hard to figure out how sailbacks like Dimetrodon got their name! Their saillike fin probably worked like a solar panel, soaking up the Sun's heat.

● The sailbacks were reptiles, and reptiles are sunbathers. They love the Sun because they are cold-blooded—they cannot keep their blood warm without the Sun's heat.

Dimetrodon

Which were the first furry animals?

Hair helps keep animals warm, so most warm-blooded animals have fur or feather coats. Scientists think the first warm-blooded furry animals were a type of reptile called the cynodont, which evolved about 250 m.y.a.

Cynognathus

What were the ruling reptiles?

Euparkeria

The ruling reptiles were the ancestors of the dinosaurs. Earlier reptiles had walked on all fours, but by 240 m.y.a. ruling reptiles such as Euparkeria were able to scurry around on two back legs—especially when chasing a tasty meal!

● One of the ways scientists find out what dinosaurs ate is by studying stony fossils of dino droppings—it's a good thing fossils aren't smelly!

Dryosaurus

Stegosaurus

Camptosauru

Compsognathus

● Fossils of more than 800 kinds of dinosaurs have been found and named, but scientists think there may have been at least twice as many.

How long did dinosaurs rule the land?

The earliest known dinosaurs appeared about 230 m.y.a., and the last ones died out about 65 m.y.a. So dinosaurs were around for a mind-boggling 165 million years!

● Brachiosaurus was tall enough to munch at the top of the highest trees.

Brachiosaurus

● All kinds of different dinosaurs evolved during their 165 million years on Earth, from the turkey-sized meat-eater Compsognathus to the gigantic plant-eater Brachiosaurus.

Allosaurus

Did dinosaurs rule the skies?

The dinosaurs did not have wings for flying. Other kinds of reptiles called pterosaurs ruled the skies in dinosaur times. Pterosaurs came in all shapes and sizes, but they all had wings. Quetzalcoatlus was the biggest—its 40-foot (12-m) wingspan made it the size of a small aircraft.

● Pterodaustro probably used its strange, bristly teeth like a sieve, to strain tiny sea creatures from the water.

Quetzalcoatlus

Rhamphorhynchus

● Scientists have found fossils that show some pterosaurs had furry bodies, like modern-day bats.

Peloneustes

● Like land reptiles, the sea reptiles breathed air. Most of them had to return to land to lay their eggs.

Elasmosaurus

● Pterosaurs' wings were leathery flaps of skin which hung from one enormously long finger on each hand.

Pterodactylus

Did dinosaurs rule the seas?

Dinosaurs were land animals, and other reptiles ruled the seas in dinosaur times. But, some of these sea reptiles looked a lot like dinosaurs— Elasmosaurus had a long neck, just like Brachiosaurus.

Pterodaustro

● At over 50 feet (15m) from nose to tail, Liopleurodon was as long as a bus!

Ichthyosaurus

Liopleurodon

● Ichthyosaurus never had to flop around on dry land. Instead of laying eggs, it gave birth to live baby Ichthyosauruses underwater.

Where did birds come from?

Dinosaurs may not have been able to fly, but scientists think that birds evolved from dinosaurs, not from pterosaurs. The earliest known feathered flyer was Archaeopteryx. It lived over 145 m.y.a., and scientists think it was a dinobird—half dinosaur and half bird.

Archaeopteryx

● Caudipteryx was another feathered dinobird, but it couldn't fly—its wings were too small.

● The duckbilled dinosaurs were gentle plant-eaters that came along after flowering plants appeared.

Edmontosaurus

When did the first flowers bloom?

Flowering plants didn't appear until about 140 m.y.a., so only the later kinds of dinosaurs would have seen and smelled them. Two of the earliest trees to blossom and fruit were magnolias and figs.

• Fossil-hunters have found part of a meat-eating dinosaur bigger than Tyrannosaurus. They've called it Giganotosaurus, which means "giant southern lizard."

Why was Tyrannosaurus king of the dinosaurs?

Tyrannosaurus

Imagine a giant with teeth as long as your hands and a mouth that's big enough to swallow you whole—that was Tyrannosaurus. It was one of the largest meat-eating land animals the world has ever known, and that's why it is called king of the dinosaurs.

• Tyrannosaurus was among the last kinds of dinosaurs to evolve, fewer than 70 m.y.a. Its name means "tyrant lizard" (a tyrant is a cruel ruler).

Were mammals around in dinosaur times?

The first mammals had probably evolved from cynodonts by about 220 m.y.a., a few million years after the first dinosaurs appeared. The earliest mammals were furry insect-eaters, not much bigger than modern-day mice.

Megazostrodon

Kamptobaator

Taeniolabis

Ptilodus

Zalambdalestes

● Megazostrodon could have sat on your hand—from its nose to the tip of its tail it only measured 4½ inch (12cm).

●One of the special things about mammals is that mothers make milk in their bodies to feed their babies.

• The babies of most of the mammals living today develop in their mother's womb. They aren't born until they're big enough to survive in the outside world.

Which babies lived in their mother's pocket?

Early mammals laid eggs, as their ancestors the reptiles had done. Over time though, other mammals evolved. These gave birth to their babies, instead of hatching them from eggs. Marsupials first appeared about 100 m.y.a. Marsupials are mammals whose newborn babies grow up in a pocketlike pouch on their mother's tummy.

Deltatheridium

• Newborn marsupials are 1 inch (2.5cm) long—no bigger than a jelly baby candy! They live in their mother's pouch until they can find their own food outside the pouch.

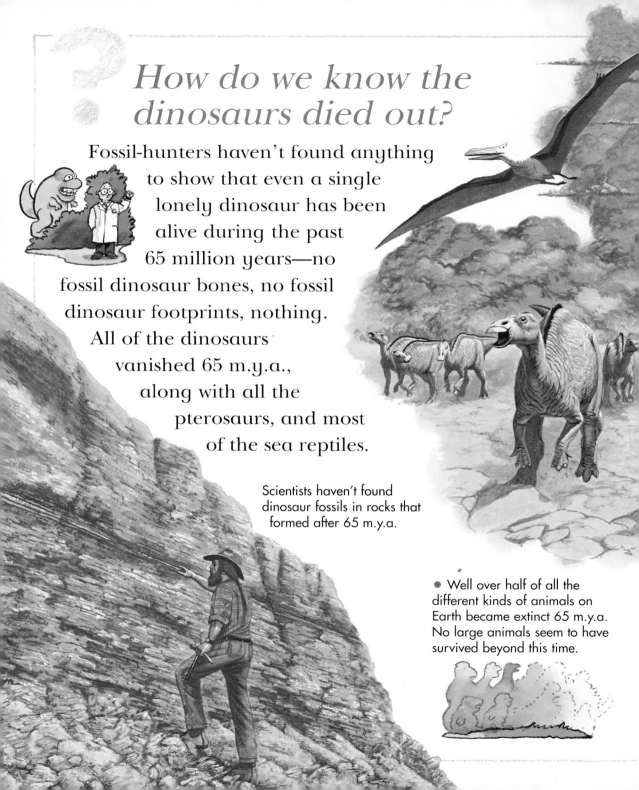

How do we know the dinosaurs died out?

Fossil-hunters haven't found anything to show that even a single lonely dinosaur has been alive during the past 65 million years—no fossil dinosaur bones, no fossil dinosaur footprints, nothing. All of the dinosaurs vanished 65 m.y.a., along with all the pterosaurs, and most of the sea reptiles.

Scientists haven't found dinosaur fossils in rocks that formed after 65 m.y.a.

● Well over half of all the different kinds of animals on Earth became extinct 65 m.y.a. No large animals seem to have survived beyond this time.

• We cannot be sure that it was the space rock that changed Earth's weather and killed off the dinosaurs. Some scientists think that exploding volcanoes sent up dust clouds to block out the Sun.

What killed the dinosaurs?

Many scientists think that the dinosaurs were wiped out after a city-sized chunk of space rock crashed into Earth 65 m.y.a. The impact was like tens of thousands of bombs exploding. Huge waves swept across the oceans and the land. Vast clouds of dust flew up into the sky, blotting out the Sun and plummeting Earth into icy darkness.

• Plants cannot grow without sunlight, so the big plant-eating animals died of cold and hunger first, and then the big meat-eaters died.

• Some people used to think that the dinosaurs died out because the mammals ate all their eggs!

• No one knows for sure why some animals survived and others didn't. Perhaps it was because they were small enough to hide in burrows.

Which animals took over from the dinosaurs?

With no meat-eating dinosaurs around to hunt them, more and more new kinds of mammals began to evolve. Most were land animals, but some took to the air and others to the seas.

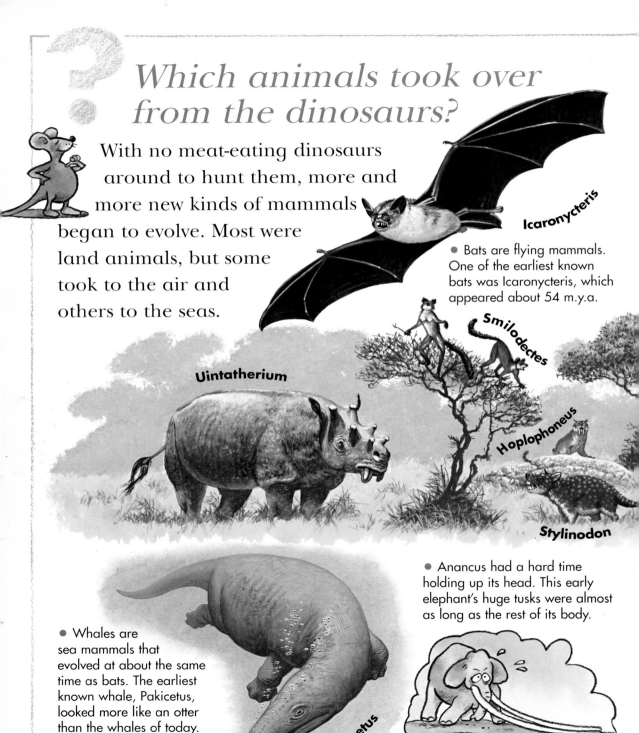

Icaronycteris

● Bats are flying mammals. One of the earliest known bats was Icaronycteris, which appeared about 54 m.y.a.

Smilodectes

Uintatherium

Hoplophoneus

Stylinodon

● Anancus had a hard time holding up its head. This early elephant's huge tusks were almost as long as the rest of its body.

● Whales are sea mammals that evolved at about the same time as bats. The earliest known whale, Pakicetus, looked more like an otter than the whales of today.

Pakicetus

When were elephants as small as pigs?

• When horses appeared about 50 m.y.a., they were tiny too. Hyracotherium had toes instead of hooves and was cat-sized—about 8 inches (20cm) high.

Elephants went through all kinds of weird and wonderful stages before they evolved into the animals we know today. When Moeritherium appeared about 40 m.y.a, it was one of the earliest elephants—and only two feet (60cm) tall!

Moeritherium

Indricotherium

Brontotherium

Protocerus

Hoplophoneus

Which cats had dagger-sized teeth?

The saber-toothed cats were named because of their massive fangs. These weren't used for eating, but for stabbing and killing their victims!

Who was Lucy?

Around 4.5 m.y.a., some new mammals appeared —the earliest humanlike creatures. They have scientific names such as Australopithecus, which means "southern ape." The fossilized skeletons of these creatures are given easy-to-say nicknames, such as Lucy.

● Lucy's fossilized skeleton was found in Africa in 1974. She was named after a Beatles song, "Lucy in the Sky with Diamonds," which was playing on the fossil-hunters' radio at the time.

Australopithecus

Homo habilis

When did humans get handy?

Homo habilis means "handy human," and these human ancestors were named because they were probably the first to use tools. They lived about 2 m.y.a., and their tools were simple stones.

Who were the first explorers?

Although all early humans evolved in Africa, Homo erectus, who appeared about 2 m.y.a., were very adventurous people. They were the first to head north out of Africa and explore Asia and Europe.

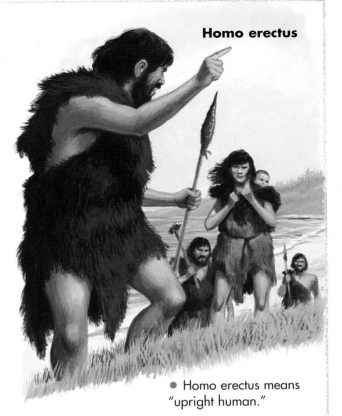

Homo erectus

● Homo erectus means "upright human."

● Homo sapiens were the first Australians. They sailed there from Southeast Asia more than 50,000 years ago.

Who were the wise humans?

Modern humans are smart, which is why our scientific name is Homo sapiens, meaning "wise human." Our closest ancestors, the first Homo sapiens, evolved in Africa almost 200,000 years ago.

Homo sapiens

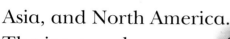

What were the ice ages?

The ice ages were long periods of time when it was so cold that snow and ice spread down from the North Pole to cover vast areas of Europe, Asia, and North America. The ice ages began about 2 m.y.a., and the last one melted away after the weather began warming up again about 12,000 years ago.

● Mammoths lived in northern lands, where their woolly coats kept them warm. The climate got too hot for them after the last Ice Age ended, and they became extinct.

Did ice age people live in caves?

They did if they could find one, but they also built huts from tree branches or from mammoth bones and tusks covered in animal skins.

● The first crops were wheat and barley, and the first farm animals were goats and sheep.

Who were the first farmers?

Farming began about 10,000 years ago, when people in the Middle East began saving the seeds of wild plants to sow as their own crops. Growing their own food meant that farmers could stay in the same place all year. They built villages, which grew into towns and then into cities. The prehistoric age was over, and with the invention of writing, modern human history had begun.

● Some of the earliest known huts were built about 400,000 years ago by Homo erectus at a place called Terra Amata, on the southern French coast.

Index